AR Book Level: 2, 8

W9-BNU-918

Lexile Level: 380

436727

By Narinder Dhami
Illustrated by Jessica Fuchs

Librarian Reviewer
Marci Peschke
Librarian, Dallas Independent School District
MA Education Reading Specialist, Stephen F. Austin State University
Learning Resources Endorsement, Texas Women's University

Reading Consultant
Elizabeth Stedem
Educator/Consultant, Colorado Springs, CO
MA in Elementary Education, University of Denver, CO

STONE ARCH BOOKS
Minneapolis   San Diego

First published in the United States in 2007
by Stone Arch Books,
151 Good Counsel Drive, P.O. Box 669,
Mankato, Minnesota 56002.
www.stonearchbooks.com

Published by arrangement with
Barrington Stoke Ltd, Edinburgh.

Library of Congress Cataloging-in-Publication Data
Dhami, Narinder.
    Grow up, Dad! / by Narinder Dhami; illustrated by Jessica Fuchs.
    p. cm. — (Pathway Books)
    Summary: When a mysterious email gives eleven-year-old Robbie the
ability to make wishes come true just as he is fighting with his father, the two
of them get a rare opportunity to relate to one another on the same level and
even face up to the school bully.
    ISBN-13: 978-1-59889-102-7 (hardcover)
    ISBN-10: 1-59889-102-2 (hardcover)
    ISBN-13: 978-1-59889-258-1 (paperback)
    ISBN-10: 1-59889-258-4 (paperback)
    [1. Fathers and sons—Fiction. 2. Wishes—Fiction. 3. Magic—Fiction.]
I. Fuchs, Jessica, ill. II. Title. III. Series.
PZ7.D54135Gro 2007
[Fic]—dc22
          2006007174

Art Director: Heather Kindseth
Graphic Designer: Kay Fraser

1 2 3 4 5 6 11 10 09 08 07 06

Printed in the United States of America

Table of Contents

Do you know what I am?

I'm a fool!

That's right.

A fool. An idiot. A loser.

I'm all of those things.

You see, I could be sitting in the sun in Florida with my mom.

But I'm not.

It all started earlier. I was here in my bedroom, and Dad was yelling at me. Nothing unusual about that. He's usually yelling at me.

"Robbie! Have you cleaned up your bedroom yet? Robbie!"

Dad was yelling at me, and he was mad. I could tell.

So what? Seems like Dad was always mad at me these days.

I pressed a button on my computer. The screen lit up.

```
Have you ever felt fed up with
your family?

Have you ever wanted a brand
new one?
```

I felt like that about my dad.

I wish there was a Dad Swap Shop.
I'd march him right down there and
trade him in for a new one.

I could hear Dad running up the
stairs. Now he was at the top.

Bang! My bedroom door suddenly
crashed open.

"Robbie, did you hear me?" Dad
asked. He was very angry. "Have you
picked up your bedroom yet?"

I didn't say a thing. I didn't have to. I
hadn't made my bed, my clothes were on
the floor, and there were CDs everywhere.
Now Dad and I were going to have a big
fight. But that was nothing new.

We were always fighting.

"You haven't done anything!" Dad said. "How many times do I have to tell you?"

"I'll do it later," I promised, keeping my eyes locked on my computer screen. I wanted to check my e-mail and see if Mom had replied to my last message.

"That's what you always say," Dad said. He stepped into the room and fell over my backpack. I tried not to smile.

"You spend too much time on that computer," Dad snapped. "Get this room picked up, Robbie. Now!"

"Later." I swung around in my chair and looked angrily at Dad.

"Now," Dad commanded.

One of us would have to give in, and it wasn't going to be me.

Just then, the doorbell rang. I slid out of my chair and ran down to see who it was.

Saved by the bell, I thought.

Dad's been like this ever since Mom left. He used to be fun, but now he's a pain. He's hardly ever at home, because he's always doing overtime at work. We never do fun stuff together anymore. He nags me all the time. "Robbie, clean your bedroom." "Robbie, do your homework." "Robbie, do this." "Robbie, do that."

I wish I'd gone to Florida with Mom and her new boyfriend.

When Mom and Dad split up, they said it was up to me to choose where I wanted to live. I could go to Florida with Mom and Scott, or I could stay here with Dad.

Now you know why I'm a fool.

I said I'd stay with Dad. I didn't like to think of him all alone, and I know he didn't want me to go. Big mistake. All Dad wanted was someone to yell at. I'm getting sick of it.

I opened the front door. My best friend Joe stood outside.

* * *

Let me explain a few things.

Truth is, Joe used to be my best friend, but right now I don't want to hang out with him anymore.

"Hi, Robbie," Joe said. He looked down at his feet. "Um, me and some of the guys are going over to the park to play soccer."

Joe and I have had a lot of fights this week. We had a big one at school yesterday. Joe said I looked at things the wrong way just because I was complaining about Dad. You know what else Joe said? He said I should give Dad a break! What does Joe know about it, anyway?

When was Dad going to give me a break? I missed Mom, and I was tired of being nagged all the time.

Joe and I stood there, looking at each other.

"Well?" Joe said at last. "Do you want to come, or not?"

I wanted to say "Yes." But, I didn't.

"No, thanks," I said.

Joe looked upset. "I guess you're going to go out with your new friends," he said.

I frowned. "What new friends?"

"Crusher Capstick and his crew," said Joe. "I saw you hanging around with them after school yesterday."

Crusher Capstick was in our class at school. He was a pain and a bully and a pest. All the teachers hated him. Most of the kids did, too. Crusher was always starting fights or talking back to the teachers or skipping school.

Still, he was cool, and he didn't care about anything or anyone. I wanted to be just like him.

"Leave me alone," I said. Then I slammed the door in Joe's face.

Nice one! Now my dad and my best friend both hated me.

My life was a mess.

Plus, it could only get worse.

What should I do? Should I stay here with Dad, or go to Florida? I didn't know anymore.

I sat down and thought it over. It didn't take me long to make up my mind. I decided to e-mail Mom and ask her to send me a ticket to Florida. I'd move in with her and Scott. Everything would be cool.

I didn't care if I ever saw Dad again. Or Joe, for that matter.

Dad wasn't going to miss me anyway. He was at work most of the time. If he wanted to nag someone, he could get a dog!

I ran upstairs to e-mail Mom. By the next week, I'd be gone. I felt a pain deep down inside me, but I knew it was for the best.

Dad had gone into his bedroom and shut the door. I was glad. I didn't want to tell him I was leaving until it was all worked out.

I sat down and opened up my e-mail. I hope my mom lets me bring the computer, I thought.

My computer was the best friend I had right now. I wasn't going to leave it behind.

I only had one new e-mail, and it wasn't from Mom. It was junk mail. For once, my junk mail looked very interesting.

CHAPTER 2

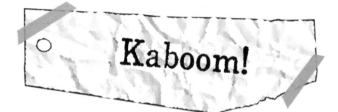

I never open junk mail. Dad always tells me to delete it in case it has a virus.

But this time I didn't press delete. I sat and looked at the message on my screen.

They were almost the same words I'd said to myself just a few moments ago. Talk about strange!

I looked at the delete key, but I didn't press it. Instead I clicked on the e-mail so I could read it all.

Kaboom!

I got a real shock. A shower of silver stars exploded on the screen. They were so bright that they lit up the whole room. I blinked.

The words fizzled around on the screen in front of me. They moved so fast that I started to feel dizzy.

Is your life a mess?

Pink and blue rockets shot all over the screen. Now, I felt really dizzy. I was so dazzled by the bright colors that I could barely read the words.

Do you think it can only get worse?

Someone tapped me on the arm.

"Oh!" I spun around.

We can help.

I hadn't heard Dad come into the room. I was so shocked, my finger slipped, and the message vanished.

But be careful what you wish for.
You just might get it!

It was good that the message vanished. I didn't want Dad to see that I'd been looking at junk mail.

Dad sounded angry. "Were you looking at junk mail?" he asked.

"No," I said.

"What have I told you?" Dad said. "You have to always delete junk mail in case it's a virus."

"I know," I said. "Will you please stop nagging me?"

"I only nag because you don't do what you're told," Dad said. "Look at this mess."

He waved his hand at the room. "I've asked you to clean your room a hundred times."

"I'll do it when I'm ready," I told him. "I've got other important things to think about."

"Like what?" asked Dad.

He bent down and picked up one of my shirts.

"You don't know how lucky you are, Robbie," he said, sitting on my bed.

It was as if he was talking to himself. "I wish I was 11 years old like you, with no problems and nothing to worry about."

"Oh yeah?" I said.

I was very angry. Did Dad think my life was really that great?

"Well, I wish you were the same age as me, too," I yelled. "Then you'd see that I've got tons of problems!"

But be careful what you wish for. You just might get it!

CHAPTER 3

I Get My Wish

There was no flash of silver light, no puff of smoke. I just felt a little dizzy. That was all.

But something had happened. Something huge.

Could this be true? I blinked. Once, twice, three times.

It was true.

Dad was still sitting on my bed. He still had my shirt in his hand.

But he wasn't Dad.

He shrunk. He was smaller than I was. His shirt and tie were too big for him.

He looked like a kid dressing up in his dad's clothes. His hair was weird, too. He always wore it short, but now it was long and messy, just like mine.

I gasped.

My dad looked like he was eleven years old.

"What's happened to me?" Dad asked in a high voice. "I feel funny. I sound funny, too!"

I gazed at him. "Look in the mirror," I said.

Dad stood up and went over to the mirror. He jumped when he saw himself.

"Is this some kind of trick, Robbie?" he asked.

I might have known Dad would blame me for what happened to him. Then I remembered the e-mail.

"Robbie!" Dad was starting to sound very upset. "Is this a joke?"

"No," I said. "You shrunk. Look at your clothes. They're too big for you."

Dad stared down at himself. His eyes were popping out of his head.

"What's going on?" he asked.

"I think you're eleven years old," I told him.

Dad looked at me as if I were crazy.

"You wanted to be eleven," I said. "Now you are."

"Don't be silly," Dad began.

Then he looked at himself, turning his head this way and that in the mirror. He shut his eyes and opened them again.

"Oh no!" he said at last. "I *am* eleven years old!" He sat down on my bed and put his head in his hands. "I'm sick! There's something very wrong with me!"

"I don't think so," I said.

How could opening the junk e-mail have done this? Wishes and magic spells were for kids.

But something odd had certainly happened to Dad.

Dad jumped up from the bed and tripped over his long jeans.

"I'd better go to the doctor," he said. He sounded upset.

"It's Saturday," I told him. "They're closed today."

"We'll go to the hospital then." Dad still looked very shocked. "You'll have to lend me some of your clothes, Robbie. I can't go like this."

I gave Dad a pair of my jeans, a t-shirt and some sneakers.

"I don't know why you're so upset," I said. "You wanted to be eleven years old again, didn't you?"

"Don't be smart, Robbie," he snapped. "I'm still your dad."

"But you're only eleven!" I said with a grin. "And you're smaller than I am!"

Dad looked at me angrily and rushed out of the room. I started to go after him.

Before I left my room, I glanced at my computer screen. Should I read that e-mail again? Would it help Dad to get back to normal?

"Don't be stupid," I told myself. "You don't believe in magic!"

Dad was in the hall. He had the car keys in his hand.

"Dad!" I said with a grin. "You can't drive to the hospital!"

Dad looked grumpy. "Why not?" he asked.

"Because you're eleven!" I was really laughing by then.

"I only look eleven," Dad replied. "Inside I'm still thirty-two. And it's miles to the hospital. We are going to take the car."

"I don't think this is a good idea," I told him as we stepped outside.

Our silver car was parked on the side of the road. Dad walked over and unlocked it.

"Get in, Robbie," he said as he slid into the driver's seat.

I got in next to him. I had to grin when I saw that Dad's feet didn't even reach the pedals!

Dad turned red. "I'll just move the seat forward," he said.

He was moving the seat when there was a tap at the window.

We both looked up.

A policeman stood looking

"I told you this wasn't a go
I said to Dad.

Dad opened the window, try
look cool.

"Hello, Officer," he said.

The policeman didn't look very happy. "What in the world are you two kids up to?" he asked. You could tell he didn't trust us.

"Well," Dad began.

I gave him a nudge.

"Ow!" said Dad.

"My brother and I are just getting something for my dad," I quickly said. I pulled out a map from under the seat. "We're going back inside now."

"But," Dad began again.

"Stop it," I said to him. "Or I'll tell Dad."

"That isn't funny, Robbie," Dad said softly, but he got out of the car anyway.

We went back to the house. The policeman stood and watched us the whole time. He walked away when we went inside and shut the door.

"Do you still think it's a good idea to take the car?" I asked.

"Maybe not," Dad said. His cheeks had turned red. "We'll walk into town and take the bus."

We started off again. It was really weird having a dad who was the same age as me.

It didn't stop him from nagging me. "Robbie, tie your shoelaces." "Robbie, don't run across the road."

It was weird being ordered around by someone the same age as me!

We were walking to the bus stop when Dad froze.

"Oh no!" he gasped.

"What?" I asked.

"Look over there," Dad said. "It's my boss, Mr. Green!"

Mr. Green was walking our way.

"Quick!" Dad grabbed my arm. "We have to hide. I can't let him see me like this!"

"Don't worry," I told Dad. "He won't know who you are."

"You might be right," Dad agreed, but he shook his head.

Mr. Green spotted us and was smiling at me. I had met him a few times before.

He seemed nice, but Dad said he was awful at the office. He told me it was Mr. Green who made him work so much overtime.

"Hello, Robbie," called Mr. Green. "Nice to see you again." He looked at Dad. "And who's this?"

"I'm, uh, one of Robbie's friends," said Dad.

"Well, nice to meet you," he said. "How's your dad, Robbie?"

"He's not too bad," I replied. "He's just not feeling like himself at the moment." I thought that was funny, but Dad didn't laugh.

Mr. Green nodded.

"Yes, your dad's working too hard," he said.

"I keep telling him to slow down, but he says he's fine."

My mouth fell open. That's not what Dad told me.

"Tell him from me to take it easy." Mr. Green waved at us and went on his way.

I turned around and looked at Dad. He was bright red.

"What's going on, Dad?" I asked. "You said you had to spend all that time at the office."

"Well," Dad mumbled. "The thing is, I need the money. We don't have the money from your mom's job anymore. That's why I've been working so much overtime."

For a moment I felt angry with myself. Of course we had less money now. Still, I felt angry with Dad, too.

"Why didn't you tell me the truth?" I asked him.

"Because it's my job to take care of things," said Dad.

"You didn't have to lie to me. I'm not a kid!"

"Yes, you are," Dad said.

"Well, so are you!" I said.

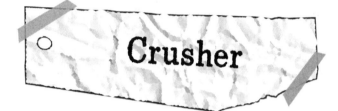

CHAPTER 4

Crusher

Dad looked really angry. I didn't know what he was going to do next. Then we heard a shout behind us.

"Robbie! Hey, Robbie!"

I looked around. Crusher Capstick and his crew were coming down the street. Crusher walked in front.

He wore his baseball cap backward, and he looked pretty cool.

"Hey, Crusher," I called back. "How's it going?"

"Crusher?" Dad said. "What kind of a name is that?"

Crusher and the others stopped in front of us and looked Dad up and down. "Who's your geeky friend, Robbie?" Crusher asked with a grin. The rest of the guys, Ed, Rocky, Kirk, and Dave, all laughed.

"This is my— ," I stopped myself. I had almost said Dad. "This is Terry."

"Please call me Mr. Carter," Dad said coldly to Crusher.

"Ooooh!" Crusher grinned. "Mr. Carter, eh? Do you hear that, guys? Well, you can call me Mr. Capstick!"

The others laughed.

I didn't like the way things seemed to be going.

"Crusher Capstick?" Dad said. "I know that name." He turned to me. "Robbie, is this the boy who's always in trouble at school? Is he a friend of yours?"

I was stuck. I didn't want Dad to know I'd been hanging around with Crusher's crew.

"Yeah, I am," said Crusher. He put his arm around me. "Robbie hangs with us. Don't you, Rob?"

"Sort of," I said. I didn't look at Dad.

"I think you and I better have a little chat, Robbie," Dad said. "I don't want you getting into trouble, too."

Crusher and the others laughed even harder.

"Listen to him!" Crusher said. "Who does he think he is? He sounds like your dad!"

"I don't want any smart mouth from you," Dad replied angrily.

Crusher stopped laughing. Oh boy, I thought to myself. Why couldn't Dad remember that he was eleven years old?

"Hey, Rob." Crusher slapped me on the back. "You don't want to hang around with this weirdo, do you? We're on our way to the old factory. Why don't you come with us?"

"Yeah, why don't you come with us?" said the others. I opened my mouth to say something. But Dad spoke first.

"The old factory?" he said with a frown. "I don't let Robbie play there. It's much too dangerous."

Crusher looked at me with a gleam in his eye. "Are you going to listen to this loser, or are you coming with us?" he asked.

"Robbie's staying right here," Dad said loudly.

I made up my mind. "I'm coming," I said.

CHAPTER 5

"Robbie, I said no!" Dad called after me as I walked off with Crusher and his crew. "Come back here!"

There was nothing he could do. I mean, he was only eleven years old! I kept walking.

"Let's run for it," Crusher yelled. "Then we can leave that boring little geek behind."

We ran down the street.

When we got to the corner, I looked back. Dad was running after us, but he was a long way behind. He wasn't as fit as he used to be. He was panting.

I felt bad. I knew I shouldn't have run off. But Dad was getting on my nerves with all that nagging.

I was going to enjoy myself for a change.

"That got rid of him!" Crusher laughed. By the time we got to the next corner, Dad was far behind.

The tall, old factory had lots of windows and doors that were all boarded up. It looked scary.

"How do we get in?" I asked.

Crusher winked at me. "Let's go around the back," he said.

At the back of the factory, one of the boards on a window was loose. We pulled it to one side and climbed through the opening.

Inside, the air was cold and damp. Garbage was everywhere.

It was dark inside and spooky. I didn't like it at all, but I tried not to show it.

"I wonder if that stupid friend of yours will follow us," Crusher said.

"He's not stupid," I said. Then I wished I hadn't said anything when Crusher turned to me.

"Okay." Crusher folded his arms. "I wonder if that weird friend of yours will follow us."

"He's not that weird," I said.

I didn't like hearing Crusher talk about my dad like that.

"You know what?" Crusher's voice was very calm, but it sent shivers up and down my spine. "You're starting to bug me."

"Yeah," said Ed, Rocky, Kirk, and Dave. "You're starting to bug us, too."

Crusher jabbed me in the chest with his finger. It hurt.

"You're acting as weird as your stupid friend," he said. "So, you have to prove that you're not."

"How?" I asked, trying to look as brave as I could.

Crusher smiled. "Well," he said, "why don't you go up to the top floor? That will show us you're not a geek."

That sounded easy. Too easy.

Until I looked around and saw that all the stairs were boarded up.

"I can't," I said. "There's no way up."

"Oh, yes, there is," Crusher replied with a grin.

He pointed at a broken drainpipe in the corner of the factory. It went right up to the roof. The others grinned.

I looked at the drainpipe. I was sure it would break if I tried to climb it.

And if I got to the top floor, it might not be safe to walk around.

What if I fell through some rotten boards?

There was no way I was going up there.

"Go on." Crusher gave me a push. "All you have to do is climb up that drainpipe, Rob."

"Robbie! Don't do it!" called a voice I knew well.

Dad was climbing in through the window.

I groaned. Now things were going to get worse.

"Robbie!" Dad rushed over to us. His face was red. "What do you think you're doing? I can't believe you'd be so stupid!"

"I wasn't going to climb it," I said.

"You're coming home with me right now," Dad went on.

He didn't trust me. What's new?

I'd never felt so annoyed in my life.

I did something I wanted to do all day. I ran at Dad and pushed him down on the dusty floor.

Then I jumped on top of him, and we started to fight!

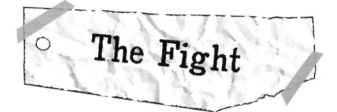

CHAPTER 6

The Fight

Crusher and his crew cheered.

"Fight! Fight!" they yelled as Dad and I rolled across the factory floor.

We were both terrible fighters.

We pushed and pulled and tugged, but neither of us could get a punch in.

Then I saw the look on Dad's face.

What on earth was I doing?

I was fighting with my eleven-year-old dad! It was crazy!

I let go of Dad and started to laugh. Dad blinked at me.

Then he grinned, and he began to laugh, too.

"What's so funny?" Crusher asked with a puzzled look.

Dad and I were both laughing too hard to answer him.

"I want to know what's going on!" Crusher demanded. Dad and I didn't answer him.

"That's it!" Crusher yelled. "Unless you tell me what's going on, you're both dead!"

"You listen to me," Dad said, walking up to Crusher. "It's about time you stopped being such a bully. I'm going to have a word with your parents, young man."

Crusher turned purple.

"Dad, you're eleven years old," I whispered in his ear. "Now there's only one way out of this."

"What's that?" asked Dad.

"Run!" I yelled.

CHAPTER 7

Soccer Star

I ran across the factory floor, dragging Dad with me.

"Get them!" Crusher shouted.

Dad and I jumped out of the window and ran for it.

Behind us we could hear Crusher and his crew yelling at each other as they all tried to climb out the window at the same time.

Dad and I dashed down the road. There was a huge recycling bin on the corner. Dad grabbed my arm and pulled me behind it.

We hid behind it and waited. A moment later we heard footsteps.

"Come on!" Crusher shouted. "They can't be far away. Robbie's dead when I get my hands on him!"

We heard them rush by us. Then there was silence.

Dad looked out from behind the bin. "They're gone," he said with a grin. "They didn't even think of looking for us back here!"

I smiled back at him. "Crusher's not very smart," I replied.

Crusher was stupid. I don't know why I ever thought he was cool.

"Brains can beat a bully every time!" Dad told me with a smile.

"Yeah," I said, "until I go to school on Monday. Crusher's going to be waiting for me."

Dad frowned. "I forgot about that," he said. "Don't worry, Robbie. We'll figure out something."

"Thanks, Dad," I said. "Think we should go home now?"

"Yes," said Dad. "Let's go through the park."

Dad and I were feeling better about each other. It still wasn't like it used to be before Mom left. But it was a start.

"I wasn't really going to climb that drainpipe," I told him.

Dad looked ashamed. "I know, son," he replied. "I was just worried, that's all. I do trust you."

"Thanks," I said.

A group of boys were playing soccer in the park.

Sam, Ben, Tom, Leroy, and Darren were all in my grade at school. My friend Joe was there, too.

"Hi," I said. Would Joe speak to me? After all, I'd been pretty mean to him.

"Hey, Robbie," said Joe with a smile. He looked at Dad. "Who's this?"

"This is my friend Terry," I said.

Joe frowned. "Have we met before?" he asked. "You look like someone I know."

Dad and I grinned at each other.

"Do you two want to play soccer with us?" Joe went on.

I thought Dad would say no.

But he smiled and nodded. "Well, maybe just for a few minutes," he said. "Come on, Robbie."

We ran across the grass to join the others. They all looked glad to see us. I'd forgotten I had so many good friends.

Dad and I played on the same team.

Dad was amazing.

He couldn't run very fast because he wasn't in very good shape, but he could do lots of tricks.

He kicked the ball between Darren's legs and passed to me. I hit the ball hard. It flew into the net.

Goal!

"Your friend's fantastic!" said Joe, as he slapped me on the back. "I wish he went to our school. He could be on our team!"

I smiled. But then I saw Crusher Capstick and his crew marching toward us.

"Hey!" Crusher shouted. "Come here, Robbie! You and that weird friend of yours!"

I stayed where I was. Dad, Joe, and the others stood next to me.

"What do you want from me, Crusher?" I asked.

"You can't hang out with me and my friends anymore, you wimp!" Crusher told me.

"Good," I said. "Anything else?"

Crusher made his hands into fists. Then he looked around at me and all my friends. He only had a few guys to back him up.

"No," Crusher said. "Just stay out of my way from now on!"

"Don't worry," I replied. "I will."

We all laughed as Crusher and his crew ran off.

"I don't think you'll have any more trouble from him!" said Dad. "Now, what about this game?"

Dad scored two goals, and we won, three to one, before we had to leave.

"Bye, Joe," I called. "See you at school on Monday."

"Okay." Joe waved at me. "Hey, my dad's joining a new soccer team at the sports center. He told me to ask your dad to join, too."

I looked at Dad. "Okay, I'll tell him," I replied.

"Are things better with him now?" Joe asked.

I laughed. "Yeah, much better!"

Soon, we were only a few blocks from our house. "You should join that soccer team," I told Dad.

"Maybe I will," said Dad. "I forgot how much I enjoy playing."

Then he added, "Look, Robbie, I know things haven't been easy since your mom left. But I'm going to try harder from now on."

"Me, too," I said. "I just wish we could get along this well when you go back to being Dad again!"

CHAPTER 8

Dad's Grown Up!

All at once I felt dizzy. I blinked and shook my head.

Dad was standing in front of me. It was Dad! He was thirty-two years old again. He looked normal, except that his jeans and t-shirt were way too small for him!

"I'm all right again!" Dad gasped. "Thank goodness."

"Do you feel okay?" I asked.

Dad nodded. "I feel fine."

"You look as if you're going to burst out of those clothes!" I laughed. He was getting some very funny looks from people on the street.

"Come on, let's go home," he said.

When we reached our house, Dad went upstairs to change and I turned my computer on. That weird e-mail had vanished from the screen.

Dad came in as I turned off my computer.

"I still don't understand how this happened," he said. "But I'm back to normal now. That's all that matters." He grinned at me. "Want to watch a video tonight and order a pizza?"

"Great!" I smiled back at him. "We haven't done that in ages."

"Things are going to be different now," Dad replied.

Just then the doorbell rang. It was Joe. "Hi," he said. "You left your wallet in the park." He handed it over.

"Why don't you stay, Joe?" Dad said. "We're having a pizza."

"Great!" Joe said with a grin. "By the way, where's your friend Terry?"

I looked at Dad. "Oh, he's around somewhere," I replied. We both started to laugh.

About the Author

Narinder Dhami's father moved from India to England in the 1950s, where he and his future wife met on a bus. Growing up, Narinder was always writing stories. She typed some of them on a pink typewriter! Narinder became a school teacher, and, after entering a writing contest, she won a computer. That convinced her to write full time. She is best known for her novelization of the hit soccer film *Bend It Like Beckham*. She now lives in Cambridge, England with her husband and five cats. She loves visiting schools and meeting her readers.

About the Illustrator

Jessica Fuchs is a designer, illustrator, and part-time animator currently living in Burbank, California, where she enjoys tea, fruit trees, and the complete lack of snow.

Glossary

commanded (kuh-MAN-did)—ordered someone to do something

dazzled (DAZ-uhld)—blinded by a bright light

drainpipe (DRAYN-pyp)—a tall pipe, usually on the outside of a building, that takes water from the roof of a building down to the ground

nagging (NAG-ing)—complaining

recycling bin (ree-SYE-kling BIN)—a large container or an enclosed space where people turn in newspapers or cardboard boxes to be used again

spine (SPYN)—backbone

Discussion Questions

1. Robbie is angry at his father. What do you think is the reason for Robbie's anger? In what ways has Robbie's life changed that might cause him to feel frustrated with his dad?

2. Why do you think Robbie turns away from his friendship with Joe?

3. In what ways are Crusher and his gang different from Robbie's other friends? Why do you think Robbie hung out with Crusher's group?

4. By the end of the story, Robbie feels differently about his father. What caused his change in attitude? How will their relationship be different from now on?

Writing Prompts

1. Robbie says that he'd like to swap his dad for a different parent. Recall a time when you were frustrated with a family member, so frustrated that you wished you might have a different family. Write about what caused your frustration and how you overcame it.

2. Crusher challenges Robbie to climb the drainpipe in order for him and his friends to trust Robbie. Write about a time when you were challenged by a friend or peer. What did you do?

3. The mysterious message on Robbie's computer was never explained. If such a message appeared on your screen, write about what you would wish for and why.

Also Published by Stone Arch Books

Dead Cool
by Peter Clover

Sammy gets more than he bargained for when he brings home his new parrot, Polly. Some of Polly's old friends, a crew of ghostly pirates, follow the bird and move in with Sammy's mystified family.

The Genie
by M. Hooper

Fiona discovers that having all her wishes granted by her very own genie might not be as great as she planned.

Living with Vampires
by Jeremy Strong

Adam is the only non-vampire in his family. His bloodsucker parents have volunteered to chaperone the school dance. Now Adam needs to make sure his parents don't turn any of his friends into zombies!

On the Run
by H. Townson

Ronnie hates sports. When he pretends to be sick on Sports Day at his school, Ronnie encounters something much scarier than the high jump.

Internet Sites

Do you want to know more about subjects related to this book? Or are you interested in learning about other topics? Then check out FactHound, a fun, easy way to find Internet sites.

Our investigative staff has already sniffed out great sites for you!

Here's how to use FactHound:

1. Visit *www.facthound.com*

2. Select your grade level.

3. To learn more about subjects related to this book, type in the book's ISBN number: **1598891022**.

4. Click the **Fetch It** button.

FactHound will fetch the best Internet sites for you!